# THE STAR WARS® COOKBOOK

## WOOKIEE PIES, CLONE SCONES, AND OTHER GALACTIC GOODIES

D0188135

BY ROBIN DAVIS AND LARA STARR
PHOTOGRAPHY BY MATTHEW CARDEN

chronicle books · san francisco

Library of Congress Cataloging-in-Publication Data available.
ISBN: 978-1-4521-0466-9

Figures and vehicles courtesy of Hasbro, Galoob, and Applause.

Heath Milk Chocolate English Toffee Bar is a registered trademark
of the Hershey Foods Corporation. Oreo is a registered trademark of
Kraft Foods, Inc.

Book design by Jennifer Tolo Pierce and Daniel Carter/Studio 212.
Concepts by Matthew Carden.
Styling by Jennifer Carden.
Typeset in Bell Gothic, Clicker, Interstate, and Univers.

Manufactured in China.

10 9 8 7 6 5 4 3 2

Chronicle Books LLC
680 Second Street, San Francisco, California 94107

www.chroniclekids.com
www.starwars.com

# Table of Contents

# Introduction

Ponder, young Jedi: Why bake a standard cookie when you can bake an ultra-chewy Wookiee Cookie—*and* use *Star Wars* cookie cutters?

The Force exists in all realms, including the kitchen. Its power is as present in the oven as it is on Dagobah. With these recipes and cookie cutters, your culinary creations will be teeming with the Force.

Some of these recipes are simple enough to make on your own and enjoy with friends. There are others requiring the help of an adult. Be sure to get your parents or other grown-ups involved. Seek the wisdom of their cooking experience.

For a Jedi with limited time, there are ample ideas here for whipping up treats in a hurry. Often, all you need is twenty minutes—about the time it takes to vanquish an ice creature or rid your ship of cable-chewing mynocks.

As you venture into the kitchen, you will want the wisdom of this cookbook and the power of the cookie cutters to help guide your way. Adventure and tastiness will be yours as you shape these recipes to all who hunger for them. Accept the challenge, young Padawan, and feel the Force!

## GETTING STARTED

Before you start cooking, you must master some essential safety steps. The kitchen is a realm of peace, yet danger lurks in the most ordinary-seeming places. The three most important rules to remember are:

**1.** Keep an adult in the kitchen at all times, especially when you use knives, the stovetop, or the oven. Adults make good company and are helpful and handy to have around. (Even Luke would have been toast without Ben Kenobi to guide and protect him.) They can reach high places, drive, use the phone, pay, and offer valuable advice. Remember, never use anything sharp or hot without an adult to guide you.

**2.** Wash your hands with soap and warm water before cooking. You remember the hideous creatures in the Mos Eisley Cantina? They are nothing compared to what are crawling around on your hands. Fight those microscopic life-forms with your best weapons: soap and water. It's a good idea to wash your hands a few times while you're cooking, too, as the germ troops are known to send in constant reinforcements.

**3.** Wash the cookie cutters in warm, soapy water before you use them the first time. To help them keep their shape, avoid putting them in the dishwasher.

The calm and perceptive mind of a Jedi warrior will enable you to prevent most mishaps in the kitchen. Use it well and follow these general guidelines:

## BE CAREFUL
### Respect the mysteries of The Force

▶ Never run in the kitchen.

▶ Keep everything—pot holders, towels, packages of ingredients, this book—away from burners on the stove. The stove can be hot even if the burners are all turned off.

▶ Dry your hands before turning on any electric switch or putting in or pulling out a plug.

▶ Wash knives and other sharp utensils one at a time. Don't drop them in a pan or bucket of soapy water—you may cut yourself when you reach in to fish them out.

▶ Lift lids on hot pots at an angle away from you, directing the rising steam away from your face.

▶ Use only dry pot holders. Wet ones will give you a steam burn when you touch the handle of a hot pot.

▶ Put a pot or pan on the stove before you turn on the heat.

▶ Turn off the heat before you remove a pot or pan from the stove.

▶ Never put out a grease fire with water. Water causes grease to splatter and can spread the fire very quickly. To put out a grease fire, smother it with a tight-fitting lid or throw handfuls of baking soda onto it.

## BE AWARE
### Cultivate the awareness of a Jedi

▶ Never leave the kitchen while something is cooking on the stove or in the oven.

▶ Keep pot handles away from the edge of the stove so no one passing by topples the pot.

▶ Always position pot handles away from other stove burners. They'll get hot and burn you when you move the pot.

▶ Remove utensils from hot pots when you're not using them, placing them on a plate or spoon holder near the stove. Metal spoons and spatulas are especially dangerous, because they'll absorb and hold the heat and burn your hand when you use them.

► Start with a clean kitchen and keep it clean as you cook. When something spills, wipe it up immediately to keep accidents from happening. If you have time, wash dishes as you go.

► Turn off the blender's motor before removing the lid.

► Put ingredients away when you're finished with them.

► Know where to find the fire extinguisher and be sure it's in working order.

► Keep the fire department number next to the phone.

The tools of a Jedi chef are powerful but simple. You probably already have everything in your kitchen. Here's an alphabetical list of what you may need.

EQUIPMENT

Aluminum foil
Baking dishes
Baking sheets
Blender*
Can opener
Candy thermometer*
Cheese grater
Colander
Cookie cutters
Cooling rack
Cutting board
Electric mixer*
Food processor*
Ice-cream scoop
Ice-cream maker
Ice-cube tray
Ice pop sticks
Knives* (one large and one small)
Measuring cups and spoons
Mixing bowls of various sizes
Paper cups
Pastry bag with round tips (#3 and #10)
Pastry brush
Plastic wrap
Potato masher
Pot holders
Rolling pin
Rubber and metal spatulas
Saucepans with lids
Sieve
Sifter
Skewers*
Skillet
Star-shaped cookie cutters
Teakettle
Toaster oven*
Toothpicks
Vegetable peeler
Wax paper
Whisk
Wooden spoons

*Use these items with extreme caution. Definitely get an adult to assist you anytime you need to use them.

Go forth, young Jedi! May your Wookiee Pies be sweet, may your C-3POatmeal Crisps be chewy, and may the Force always be with you!

# Breakfasts

# Princess Leia Danish Dos

## INGREDIENTS

| | |
|---|---|
| 1 | tablespoon butter, plus more for greasing baking sheet |
| | All-purpose flour for dusting work surface |
| 1 | package (10 ounces) refrigerated pizza dough |
| 2 | tablespoons granulated sugar |
| $1\frac{1}{2}$ | teaspoons ground cinnamon |
| 1 | tablespoon milk |
| $\frac{1}{3}$ | cup confectioners' sugar, sifted |
| $\frac{1}{4}$ | teaspoon vanilla extract |

1. Preheat the oven to 350°F. Lightly grease a baking sheet.
2. Put the 1 tablespoon butter in a small saucepan. Set the pan on the stove and switch on the heat to low. When the butter has melted, turn off the heat.
3. Lightly flour a work surface. Unroll the pizza dough on top of the flour. Using a pastry brush, brush the melted butter over the surface of the dough.
4. Put the granulated sugar and cinnamon in a small bowl. Stir with a small spoon until well mixed. Sprinkle the cinnamon-sugar mixture over the dough, leaving a $\frac{1}{2}$-inch border on all sides.
5. Starting at a long side, roll up the dough into a log. Using your fingertips, pinch the seam together to seal.
6. Using a knife, cut the log crosswise into 1-inch-thick slices. Put the slices, cut-side up, onto the greased baking sheet.
7. Using pot holders, put the baking sheet in the preheated oven. Bake until golden brown, about 20 minutes. Carefully transfer the baking sheet to the cooling rack. Cool 5 minutes. With a spatula, transfer rolls to the cooling rack and cool 5 minutes more.
8. Put the milk and confectioners' sugar in a small bowl. Stir with the spoon until a smooth frosting forms. Stir in the vanilla. Using a butter knife, spread frosting over the tops of the cinnamon rolls.
**Makes about 10 rolls.**

# Tosche Station Toast

Before heading out to Tosche Station for a new power converter, fortify yourself with this tasty toast.

### INGREDIENTS

| | |
|---|---|
| 4 | eggs |
| 1 | cup milk, plus 1 tablespoon, at room temperature |
| 1 | teaspoon vanilla extract |
| 8 | ounces cream cheese, at room temperature |
| 1 | tablespoon granulated sugar |
| $1/2$ | teaspoon ground cinnamon |
| 8 | slices large sturdy sandwich bread (such as buttermilk, potato, or sourdough) |
| $1/4$ | cup unsalted butter |
| | Confectioners' sugar and/or maple syrup for serving |

**1.** Preheat the oven to 375°F.

**2.** Mix the eggs, the 1 cup milk, and vanilla in a shallow bowl and set aside. In another bowl, mix the cream cheese, remaining 1 tablespoon milk, granulated sugar, and cinnamon with a rubber spatula until well blended. Spread the cream cheese mixture onto four of the bread slices. Top each with another slice of bread and press together. Cut the sandwiches in half, or cut out shapes with the cookie cutters.

**3.** Soak each of the sandwiches in the egg mixture for about 1 minute on each side.

**4.** Place a large ovenproof skillet on the stove and switch on the heat to medium, and melt the butter. Let the excess egg batter drain off of the sandwiches, then add them to the pan. Cook 2 to 3 minutes on each side, until golden brown. Turn off the heat. Using pot holders, carefully transfer the skillet to the oven and bake until the toasts are puffed and golden, 8 to 10 minutes. Serve warm with confectioners' sugar and/or maple syrup.

**Makes 4 toasts.**

# Clone Scones

This army of scones will attack your mouth with buttery yumminess.

## INGREDIENTS

|  |  |  |  |
|---|---|---|---|
|  | Butter for greasing baking sheet | $3/4$ | cup unsalted butter, cold |
| 3 | cups all-purpose flour, plus more for dusting work surface | $3/4$ | cup raisins |
|  |  | 1 | cup milk, plus 1 tablespoon, at room temperature |
| $1/2$ | cup oats |  |  |
| $1/3$ | cup packed brown sugar | 2 | tablespoons granulated sugar |
| $2 1/2$ | teaspoons baking powder |  |  |
| $1/2$ | teaspoon baking soda | $1/2$ | teaspoon ground cinnamon |
| $1/2$ | teaspoon salt |  |  |

1. Preheat the oven to 400°F. Lightly grease a baking sheet.

2. In a large bowl, place the 3 cups flour, oats, brown sugar, baking powder, baking soda, and salt and mix on medium speed with an electric mixer until blended. Slice the butter into tablespoon-size pieces and distribute over the dry ingredients. Mix at low speed until the mixture resembles coarse meal. Add the raisins and mix briefly until the ingredients are just combined.

3. Add the 1 cup milk and mix until the dough holds together. Gather the dough into a ball with floured hands. Pat the ball about $1/2$ inch thick on a floured work surface. Cut out shapes with the cookie cutters, dipping the cutter into flour between each cut. Gather the scraps, pat, and continue cutting.

4. Transfer the shapes to the greased baking sheet. Bake until the scones are set and golden, 12 to 15 minutes.

5. While the scones are baking, mix the remaining 1 tablespoon milk with the granulated sugar and cinnamon. Using pot holders, remove the scones from the oven and brush them with the glaze while still hot. Serve warm or at room temperature.

**Makes about 16 scones.**

# Landonuts

These chocolate donuts are a sweet treat.

## INGREDIENTS

| | |
|---|---|
| 2$\frac{1}{2}$ cups all-purpose flour (spooned and leveled), plus more for dusting work surface | $\frac{3}{4}$ cup buttermilk, at room temperature |
| 1$\frac{1}{2}$ cups cocoa powder | 4 tablespoons butter, melted |
| 2 teaspoons baking powder | 2 eggs, at room temperature |
| $\frac{1}{2}$ teaspoon baking soda | 1 cup confectioners' sugar |
| $\frac{1}{2}$ teaspoon salt | Vegetable oil, for frying |
| 1 cup granulated sugar | |

**1.** In a large bowl, combine the 2$\frac{1}{2}$ cups flour, 1 cup of the cocoa powder, baking powder, baking soda, and salt in a large bowl. In a medium bowl, add the granulated sugar, buttermilk, melted butter, and eggs and whisk to combine. Stir the buttermilk mixture into the flour mixture with a wooden spoon and mix until a smooth dough forms. Chill the dough for 15 to 20 minutes.

**2.** Pat the dough flat on a floured work surface, and sprinkle the top with flour. Roll out the dough $\frac{1}{3}$ inch thick with a rolling pin. Using the cookie cutters, cut the dough into shapes, then re-roll the dough and cut the scraps into shapes. Let the cut shapes sit for 10 minutes.

**3.** Mix the remaining $\frac{1}{2}$ cup of cocoa powder and the confectioners' sugar in a shallow bowl. Line a baking sheet with several layers of paper towel.

**4.** In a large, heavy pot, add 2 inches of oil and place the pot on the stove. Switch on the heat to medium high. Clip a candy thermometer to the side of the pot. With adult help, heat the oil until it reads 350°F on the thermometer. Fry 2 to 3 donuts at a time for 2 minutes. Turning with a slotted spoon or tongs, fry for 3 more minutes. Transfer the doughnuts to the towel-lined baking sheet and let rest for 5 minutes. Toss the slightly cooled doughnuts in the cocoa sugar. Serve warm or at room temperature.
**Makes about 24 donuts.**

# Amidala Omelettes

When she's dressed for formal state occasions, Padmé Amidala wears an impressive costume of red, black, and gold—the same colors captured in this hearty breakfast dish.

## INGREDIENTS

| | |
|---|---|
| 6 | eggs, at room temperature |
| 1/4 | cup milk, at room temperature |
| 1 | cup grated mozzarella cheese |
| 1 | large red bell pepper, diced |
| 1/2 | cup pitted black olives, chopped |
| 1/2 | teaspoon salt |
| 1/2 | teaspoon pepper |
| | Vegetable-oil cooking spray |

**1.** Preheat the oven to 250°F.

**2.** Whisk together the eggs and milk in a large mixing bowl until well combined and no streaks remain. Add the cheese, bell pepper, olives, salt, and pepper and mix to incorporate. Transfer 2 cups of the mixture to a glass measuring cup with a spout.

**3.** Place a large nonstick skillet on the stove and switch on the heat to medium. With adult help, place the 3 cookie cutters in the pan. Spray the pan and the inside of the cutters with vegetable-oil cooking spray. Pour the egg mixture into the cookie cutters, filling them about half full. Cover the skillet and cook until the eggs are set, about 5 minutes. Switch off the heat.

**4.** Carefully remove the cookie cutters from the pan using tongs, leaving the omelettes in place. Remove the omelettes from the pan with a spatula, transfer to a platter or baking sheet, and keep warm in a low oven. Repeat with the rest of the egg mixture.

**Makes 4 servings.**

# Beverages

Hoth Chocolate
Yoda Soda
Jawa Jive Milkshakes
Midi-chlorian Concoction

# Hoth Chocolate

The Rebellion's hidden Echo Base on the ice planet Hoth was freezing! Sometimes the Rebels wished they could just warm up with a mug of this Hoth chocolaty drink.

## INGREDIENTS

| | |
|---|---|
| 1 | cup milk |
| 2 | heaping teaspoons sugar |
| 1 | heaping teaspoon cocoa powder |
| $1/8$ | teaspoon vanilla extract |
| | Small marshmallows (optional) |

**1.** Pour the milk into a small saucepan. Add the sugar, cocoa powder, and vanilla to the milk. Stir vigorously with a whisk until the sugar and cocoa dissolve.
**2.** Place the pan on the stove and switch on the heat to medium. Watch for tiny bubbles to appear along the edge of the pan, then immediately remove the pan from the heat.
**3.** Carefully pour into the mug and serve immediately with marshmallows, if desired.
**Makes 1 serving.**

# Yoda Soda

INGREDIENTS

3  limes

3  tablespoons sugar, or more to taste

1  cup sparkling water

1  scoop lime sherbet or sorbet

**1.** Place 1 lime on the cutting board and cut it in half. Squeeze the juice from each half into a measuring cup. Repeat with the remaining limes until you have ¼ cup juice.
**2.** Put the lime juice and 3 tablespoons sugar in a small pitcher. Stir with a wooden spoon until the sugar dissolves. Add the sparkling water and stir until mixed. Taste and add more sugar, if desired.
**3.** Using an ice-cream scoop, scoop up the sherbet and drop it into a tall glass. Pour in the lime water. Serve immediately.
**Makes 1 serving.**

Variation: You can substitute rainbow sherbet or lemon sorbet for the lime sherbet.

# Jawa Jive Milkshakes

Jawas are famous for scavenging abandoned ships, droids, and scrap metal. When they get together at giant swap meets, they allegedly serve these delicious shakes.

## CHOCOLATE-BANANA

2 cups vanilla ice cream or frozen yogurt

1 banana, peeled and broken into pieces

1/2 cup milk

1/4 cup chocolate syrup

1/2 cup crushed Heath® Bars (optional)

## VANILLA AND PEANUT BUTTER

1 cup vanilla ice cream or frozen yogurt

1 teaspoon vanilla extract

1/2 cup milk

1/4 cup creamy peanut butter

1/2 cup peanut butter chips

## SUPER STRAWBERRY

2 cups strawberry ice cream or frozen yogurt

1 cup frozen strawberries

1/2 cup milk

1/2 cup white chocolate chips (optional)

## DOUBLE CHOCOLATE

2 cups chocolate ice cream or frozen yogurt

1/2 cup milk

1/4 cup chocolate syrup

1/2 cup crushed chocolate sandwich cookies (optional)

1. Select the milkshake you want to make. Assemble the ingredients for your recipe. (Tip: The best way to crush the cookies or candy bar is to put them in a clean, sturdy plastic bag and roll a rolling pin back and forth over them.)
2. Put all the ingredients into a blender.
3. Put the lid on the blender. Make sure it fits tightly. Turn on the blender first at low speed, then increase to high speed. Blend until smooth, 1 to 2 minutes.
4. Pour the milkshake into 2 glasses. Serve each shake with a spoon and a straw.

**Makes 2 milkshakes.**

# Midi-chlorian Concoction

For a midi-chlorian count that's off the charts, we recommend a healthy helping of this tasty shake.

INGREDIENTS

| | |
|---|---|
| 1 | banana |
| $^1/_4$ | cup creamy peanut butter |
| 1 | teaspoon cocoa powder |
| 2 | teaspoons sugar |
| $1^1/_2$ | cups milk |

1. Slice the banana into a blender.
2. Add the remaining ingredients and blend 1 minute, or until smooth.
3. Serve in two chilled glasses.
**Makes 2 servings.**

# Snacks and Sides

# Wampa Snow Cones

Luke was imprisoned by a ferocious wampa on the ice planet Hoth, and held captive in the creature's frozen lair. Narrowly escaping with his life, some believe Luke also made off with the wampa's secret snow cone recipe.

## INGREDIENTS

| | |
|---|---|
| 2 | cups fresh or thawed frozen blueberries |
| ¼ | cup water |
| 1 | tablespoon sugar |

**1.** Put the blueberries in a bowl. Mash them with a fork until there's a lot of liquid.

**2.** Hold a strainer over a small glass baking dish and pour the mashed berries into a sieve. Press the berries with a fork to push through as much liquid as possible.

**3.** Add the water and sugar to the blueberry juice. With a wooden spoon, stir until the sugar dissolves. Put the dish in the freezer.

**4.** After 30 minutes take the dish out of the freezer. Stir the mixture with a fork to break up the crystals. Return the dish to the freezer for another 30 minutes.

**5.** Remove the dish again and break up the crystals a second time. Return to the freezer and freeze until firm, about 4 hours.

**6.** Remove the dish from the freezer. Using the fork, scrape the mixture into small crystals. Quickly scoop the crystals into small paper cups and serve right away.

**Makes 2 servings.**

Variation: Replace the blueberries, water, and sugar with a bottled fruit juice or drink such as apple juice, lemonade, or punch. Follow the directions for freezing and scraping the crystals.

# Biscuit Fistos

Kit Fisto's green skin may look creepy, but he's a proud Jedi. These green-tinted biscuits may also give you pause, but they have a fresh pesto flavor that is out of this world.

## INGREDIENTS

| | |
|---|---|
| 2 | cups all-purpose flour, plus more for dusting work surface |
| 2 | teaspoons baking powder |
| $1/2$ | teaspoon baking soda |
| $1/4$ | teaspoon salt |
| $1/3$ | cup vegetable shortening or butter |
| $1/2$ | cup store-bought basil pesto |
| $3/4$ | cup buttermilk, at room temperature |

**1.** Preheat the oven to 450°F.

**2.** Pulse the 2 cups flour, baking powder, baking soda, and salt in the bowl of a food processor once or twice to blend. Add the shortening or butter and pesto and pulse until the mixture resembles coarse crumbs. Add the buttermilk and pulse until the dough just holds together.

**3.** Turn the dough onto a lightly floured surface. Knead gently 10 to 12 times. Pat until $1/2$ inch thick. Cut out shapes with the cookie cutters, dipping the cutters into flour between cuts. Gather the dough scraps, pat again, and continue cutting. Place the biscuits on an ungreased baking sheet. Bake until golden, 8 to 10 minutes.

**Makes 12 biscuits.**

# Jawa Jigglers

These deep dark little treats wiggle and jiggle, just like a scurrying Jawa.

INGREDIENTS

| 4 | cups purple grape juice or pomegranate juice |
| Four | 1/4-ounce envelopes unflavored gelatin |
| 2 | tablespoons sugar |

**1.** Pour 1 cup of the juice into a large bowl. Sprinkle the gelatin evenly over the juice. Let sit for 10 minutes to soften. Heat the remaining 3 cups of juice and the sugar until simmering. Add the hot juice to the gelatin mixture and stir to combine.

**2.** Pour the mixture into a 9-by-13-inch pan. Chill for at least 3 hours, or overnight.

**3.** Dip the bottom of the pan in hot water. Cut out shapes with the cookie cutters.

**Makes about 16 jigglers.**

# Obi-Wan Tons

INGREDIENTS

One 12-ounce package egg roll wrappers

Olive oil

Assorted toppings: sesame seeds, poppy seeds, garlic powder, onion powder, seasoned salt, Parmesan cheese

**1.** Preheat the oven to 375°F.
**2.** Place an egg roll wrapper on a flat surface. Cut a shape with a cookie cutter, or cut into quarters. Continue with the rest of the wrappers in the package.
**3.** Brush a baking sheet with olive oil. Place the wrappers on the sheet, without overlapping. Brush with olive oil and sprinkle on the toppings. Bake until golden brown, about 5 to 6 minutes.
**Makes about 20 wontons.**

# Jedi Juice Pops

INGREDIENTS

14    small fresh or frozen strawberries

1¼ cups fruit juice, such as orange, cranberry,
      apple, fruit punch, or lemonade

**1.** If you are using fresh strawberries, cut off their stems with a
small knife. Place 1 strawberry in each ice cube compartment of
an ice-cube tray. Fill the ice-cube tray with the juice.
**2.** Put the tray in the freezer and freeze until almost firm, about
2 hours.
**3.** Push an ice pop stick (or a toothpick) into the center of each
cube, through the strawberry. Return to the freezer and freeze until
firm, about 1 hour longer.
**4.** Pop out the juice bars and eat!
**Makes 14 pops.**

Variation: You can use banana slices, seedless grapes, or orange
segments cut into chunks instead of strawberries.

# Cookies and Sweets

# Wookiee Cookies

## INGREDIENTS

| | |
|---|---|
| 2¼ | cups all-purpose flour |
| 1 | teaspoon baking soda |
| 1 | teaspoon salt |
| 1 | teaspoon ground cinnamon |
| 1 | cup unsalted butter, at room temperature, plus more for greasing baking sheet |
| 1 | cup packed brown sugar |
| ½ | cup granulated sugar |
| 2 | large eggs |
| 1½ | teaspoons vanilla extract |
| 1 | cup milk chocolate chips |
| 1 | cup semisweet chocolate chips |

**1.** Preheat the oven to 375°F.

**2.** Put the flour, baking soda, salt, and cinnamon in a mixing bowl. Stir with the wooden spoon until well mixed. Set aside.

**3.** Put the 1 cup butter, brown sugar, and granulated sugar in another mixing bowl. Using the electric mixer set on high speed, beat together until well blended and creamy, about 3 minutes. (You can do this with a wooden spoon, but it will take longer.) Beat in the eggs and vanilla extract. Add the flour mixture and stir with a wooden spoon until blended. Stir in the chocolate chips.

**4.** Scoop up a rounded tablespoonful of the dough and drop onto greased baking sheets. Repeat until you have used up all the dough. Be sure to leave about 1 inch between the cookies because they spread as they bake.

**5.** Using pot holders, put the baking sheets in the oven. Bake until golden brown, about 10 minutes.

**6.** Again, using pot holders, remove the baking sheets from the oven. Lift the cookies from the baking sheets with a spatula, and place on cooling racks. Let cool completely.

**Makes about 3 dozen cookies.**

# Bossk Brownies

Bossk the bounty hunter never caught his quarry, Han Solo and Chewbacca. Perhaps he was distracted by these delicious brownies.

## INGREDIENTS

| | |
|---|---|
| 1/2 | cup unsalted butter, at room temperature, plus more for greasing baking dish |
| 2/3 | cup all-purpose flour |
| 1/2 | cup unsweetened cocoa powder |
| 1/2 | teaspoon baking powder |
| 1/2 | teaspoon salt |
| 1/2 | cup packed brown sugar |
| 1/2 | cup granulated sugar |
| 2 | large eggs |
| 1 | teaspoon vanilla extract |
| 1/2 | cup white chocolate or butterscotch chips |

1. Preheat the oven to 350°F. Grease an 8-inch square baking dish.
2. Put the flour, cocoa powder, baking powder, and salt in a small bowl. Stir with a wooden spoon until well mixed. Set aside.
3. Put the 1/2 cup butter, brown sugar, and granulated sugar in a large bowl. Using the electric mixer set on high speed, beat together until well blended and creamy, about 3 minutes. (You can do this with the wooden spoon, but it will take longer.) Beat in the eggs and vanilla. Add the flour mixture and stir with the wooden spoon until blended. Stir in the white chocolate or butterscotch chips.
4. Pour into the prepared baking dish and smooth the top with a rubber spatula.
5. Using pot holders, put the baking dish in the oven. Bake until a toothpick inserted into the center comes out clean, about 25 minutes.
6. Again using pot holders, transfer the dish to the cooling rack. Let cool completely.

**Makes about 16 brownies.**

# Death Star Popcorn Balls

Like the Empire's deadly Death Star, making popcorn balls can be very dangerous. Do not dare to make them without the help of an adult.

## INGREDIENTS

| | | | |
|---|---|---|---|
| $1/3$ | cup popcorn kernels | 1 | teaspoon vinegar |
| 3 | cups sugar | 1 | teaspoon vanilla extract |
| $1^1/2$ | cups water | | Butter or vegetable |
| $1/2$ | cup light corn syrup | | shortening for |
| $1/2$ | tablespoon salt | | greasing hands |

1. Get an adult to help you with this recipe!
2. Pop the corn using whatever method you prefer.
3. Put the sugar, water, corn syrup, and salt in the saucepan. Stir well with a wooden spoon. With adult help, clip a candy thermometer on the side of the pan. Set the pan on the stove and switch on the heat to low. Add the vinegar and vanilla and cook, stirring constantly, until the thermometer reads 270°F.
4. Get an adult to carefully pour the hot sugar mixture over the popcorn and toss using 2 large spoons to coat every kernel. Allow to cool slightly.
5. Rub butter or vegetable shortening on your hands so the popcorn won't stick to them. Then scoop up enough popcorn to form a ball about the size of a baseball.
6. Shape the ball with your hands.

Makes 2 or 3 popcorn balls.

# R2-D2 Treats

R2-D2 never eats, or so it seems. These frozen treats were discovered in a freezer at the abandoned Rebel base on Hoth. Did they belong to R2-D2? We can only guess . . .

## INGREDIENTS

| | |
|---|---|
| $1/2$ | cup white chocolate chips |
| 1 | banana |
| 2 | tablespoons chopped peanuts |
| 2 | pieces chocolate-covered wafer candy bar |

1. Line a baking sheet with wax paper.
2. Put the chocolate chips in a small, heavy saucepan. Put the pan on the stove and switch on the heat to low. Stir constantly until the chocolate is melted and smooth. Remove from heat and set aside.
3. Peel the banana. Put on a cutting board and cut into 4 equal pieces.
4. Place the peanuts in a small bowl. Break apart the 2 pieces of chocolate-covered wafer candy bar. Cut each piece in half and set aside.
5. Dip 1 banana piece in the melted chocolate. Dip the top, front, and back of the banana piece into the peanuts.
6. Place the banana piece nut-side up on the lined baking sheet. Press the 2 chocolate-covered wafer candy bar pieces along either side of the banana.
7. Repeat steps 5 and 6 with the remaining banana pieces.
8. Place the baking sheet in the freezer until the chocolate hardens, about 15 minutes. Serve straight from the freezer.
**Makes 1 or 2 treats.**

# Sandtrooper Sandies

## INGREDIENTS

| | |
|---|---|
| $3/4$ cup butter, at room temperature | $1/4$ teaspoon salt |
| $1^1/4$ cups granulated sugar | Vegetable oil for greasing baking sheet |
| 2 eggs | Confectioners' sugar |
| 1 teaspoon vanilla extract | |
| 2 cups all-purpose flour, plus more for dusting work surface | |

**1.** Put the butter in a bowl. With an electric mixer set on high speed, beat the butter until soft and light in color.

**2.** Gradually add the granulated sugar in a slow, steady stream, and beat until creamy and lemon yellow. Then add the eggs 1 at a time, beating well after each addition. Add the vanilla and stir just until blended.

**3.** Put the 2 cups flour and salt into a sifter and sift them into a small bowl. Slowly add the flour mixture to the butter mixture, beating it in with the electric mixer on low speed until it is fully incorporated. The dough will become very stiff and you may have to knead the last bit of flour in by hand. With your hands, pat the dough into a ball and flatten the ball into a thick disk. Wrap the dough in plastic wrap and chill in the refrigerator for 1 hour.

**4.** Preheat the oven to 400°F. Lightly oil a baking sheet.

**5.** Remove dough from the refrigerator and unwrap. Dust your work surface with flour. With a rolling pin, roll out the dough $1/4$ inch thick.

**6.** Using cookie cutters of any shape you like, cut cookies out of the dough. Carefully transfer the cookies to the oiled baking sheet, leaving a little space around each one. Gather up any dough scraps, roll them out again, and cut out more cookies.

**7.** Slip baking sheet into the oven and bake until cookies just begin to brown, 8 to 10 minutes. Using pot holders, carefully remove the baking sheet from the oven. Transfer the cookies to cooling racks with a spatula and allow them to cool. Sift a little confectioners' sugar over the cookies.

**Makes about 3 dozen cookies.**

# Hideous Sidious Sorbet

Here's the scoop: Icy and cold as the Sith Lord himself, this sorbet is surprisingly sweet. But like Sidious, it has the power to melt away without a trace.

INGREDIENTS

| | |
|---|---|
| 1/2 | cup sugar |
| 3 | cups frozen blackberries, drained |
| 1/2 | cup berry Italian soda syrup (any kind of berry will work) |
| 2 | tablespoons fresh lemon juice |
| 1/2 | cup heavy cream |
| 1 | sheet grape or berry fruit leather |

**1.** In a blender, purée the sugar and berries until smooth. Strain the purée to remove seeds. Rinse the blender, and pour the berry purée, syrup, lemon juice, and heavy cream into it. Blend until mixed.
**2.** Freeze in an ice-cream maker according to the manufacturer's instructions.
**3.** To serve, place 2 scoops of the sorbet in a bowl. Cut the fruit leather into 4 equal pieces. Drape the fruit leather over the sorbet, 1 piece per bowl, to resemble Darth Sidious's hood. Serve immediately.
**Makes 4 servings.**

# Darth Vader Dark Chocolate Sundaes

Some speculate that Darth Vader was lured to the Dark Side by these Dark Chocolate Sundaes.

### INGREDIENTS

| | |
|---|---|
| $1/2$ | cup bottled hot fudge sauce |
| 1 | quart chocolate ice cream |
| $1/2$ | cup whipped cream |
| 4 | tablespoons chopped nuts |
| 4 | teaspoons chocolate chips or chocolate sprinkles |

**1.** Put the hot fudge sauce in a small, heavy saucepan. Put the pan on the stove and switch on the heat to low. Stir constantly until the sauce is melted and smooth. Remove from the heat.
**2.** Set out 4 bowls. Put 2 scoops of ice cream into each bowl.
**3.** Top each serving with about 2 tablespoons hot fudge. Top with about 2 tablespoons of the whipped cream and sprinkle each serving with 1 tablespoon nuts and 1 teaspoon chocolate chips or sprinkles. Serve immediately.
**Makes 4 servings.**

Variations: You can use any flavor ice cream or sauce that you like. Other toppings besides peanuts might include mini marshmallows, fresh berries, or shredded coconut.

# Mos Eisley Morsels

## INGREDIENTS

| | | | | |
|---|---|---|---|---|
| | Butter for greasing baking dish | | $1/2$ | teaspoon ground cloves |
| 2 | cups all-purpose flour | | $1/4$ | teaspoon salt |
| 2 | teaspoons baking powder | | 3 | large bananas |
| $1/2$ | teaspoon baking soda | | 1 | large egg |
| $1^1/2$ | teaspoons ground cinnamon | | 2 | tablespoons vegetable oil |
| 1 | teaspoon ground nutmeg | | 2 | teaspoons vanilla extract |

1. Preheat the oven to 375°F.
2. Lightly grease an 8-inch square baking dish.
3. Put the flour, baking powder, baking soda, cinnamon, nutmeg, cloves, and salt into a sifter. Sift the ingredients into a large bowl.
4. In another large bowl, thoroughly mash the bananas with a fork or potato masher. Add the egg, vegetable oil, and vanilla, and stir until well blended.
5. Add the flour mixture and, with a rubber spatula, mix the wet and dry ingredients together until just combined.
6. Pour the batter into the prepared baking dish and smooth the top of the batter with the spatula.
7. Using pot holders, place the baking dish in the oven and bake until a toothpick inserted into the center comes out clean, 30 to 35 minutes. Using pot holders, transfer the dish to a cooling rack. Cut into squares.
**Makes 12 morsels.**

Variations: The morsels in the picture are topped with an extra mashed banana. If desired, mash a banana in a separate bowl, and spread on squares just before eating. Do not top the morsels with mashed banana unless you're going to eat them right away!

# C-3POatmeal Crisps

Proper protocol is to dunk these crispy cookies in milk or hot chocolate.

## INGREDIENTS

| | |
|---|---|
| 1 | cup butter, at room temperature, plus more for greasing baking sheet |
| 3/4 | cup packed brown sugar |
| 1 | large egg |
| 2 | teaspoons vanilla extract |
| 3/4 | teaspoon salt |
| 1/2 | teaspoon baking powder |
| 1 | teaspoon ground cinnamon |
| 1 | cup rolled oats |
| 2 1/2 | cups all-purpose flour, plus more for dusting work surface |

1. Put the 1 cup butter and brown sugar in a mixing bowl. Using the electric mixer set on high speed, beat together until well blended and creamy. Add the egg and vanilla and beat until incorporated. In a separate bowl, mix together the salt, baking powder, cinnamon, oats, and 2 1/2 cups flour. Add the dry ingredients to the butter mixture and beat until the dough holds together.
2. Divide the dough into 2 balls. Wrap each ball in plastic wrap, and flatten into a disk. Refrigerate for 1 hour, or overnight.
3. Preheat the oven to 350°F. Grease a baking sheet.
4. On a floured surface, use a rolling pin to roll out each disk of chilled dough about 1/4 inch thick, and cut shapes out of the dough with the cookie cutters. Place on the greased baking sheet. Gather up any dough scraps, roll them out again, and cut out more cookies. Bake until the tops are golden, 14 to 16 minutes.
5. Using pot holders, remove the baking sheet from the oven and let the cookies sit for 5 minutes, then remove to the cooling rack with the spatula to cool completely.
**Makes about 4 dozen cookies.**

# Chocolate Chewies

These super-chocolaty cookies would make Chewbacca roar with joy!

### INGREDIENTS

| | |
|---|---|
| 3 | cups all-purpose flour, plus more for dusting work surface |
| $3/4$ | teaspoon salt |
| $1/2$ | teaspoon baking powder |
| 1 | cup butter, at room temperature, plus more for greasing baking sheet |
| $1^1/2$ | cups sugar |
| 2 | large eggs |
| 1 | teaspoon vanilla extract |
| $2/3$ | cup unsweetened cocoa |

**1.** Whisk the 3 cups flour, salt, and baking powder in a bowl and set aside. In a separate bowl, beat the 1 cup butter, sugar, eggs, vanilla, and cocoa with the electric mixer until well combined. Gradually add the flour mixture and mix until smooth. Wrap the dough in plastic wrap, flatten into a disk, and chill for at least 1 hour or overnight.

**2.** Preheat the oven to 350°F. Grease a baking sheet.

**3.** On a floured surface, use a rolling pin to roll out the chilled dough about ¼ inch thick. Cut out shapes with the cookie cutters. Place on the greased baking sheet. Gather up any dough scraps, roll them out again, and cut out more cookies. Bake until the edges look firm, 10 to 12 minutes.

**4.** Using pot holders, remove the baking sheet from the oven and let the cookies sit for 5 minutes, then remove to the cooling rack with the spatula to cool completely.

**Makes about 4 dozen cookies.**

# 3-Layer Admiral Ack-bars

It's not a trap! These moist bars are great for dessert or an after-school snack.

## INGREDIENTS

$1^1/2$ cups butter, at room temperature, plus more for greasing pan

3 cups rolled oats

1 cup brown sugar

1 cup granulated sugar

3 cups all-purpose flour

1 teaspoon salt

2 teaspoons baking powder

1 teaspoon ground ginger

2 cups apricot preserves

**1.** Preheat the oven to 350°F. Line a 9-by-13-inch baking pan with aluminum foil and lightly grease the foil.

**2.** Place the oats, brown sugar, granulated sugar, flour, salt, baking powder, and ginger in a large bowl and mix with the wooden spoon to combine. Add the $1^1/2$ cups butter and mix until crumbly.

**3.** Pour half of the mixture into the foil-lined pan and press down with your fingers until flat and even. Spread the apricot preserves over the dough. Sprinkle the rest of the dough evenly over the preserves and pat down.

**4.** Bake until the top is lightly golden, 30 or 40 minutes. Using pot holders, remove to the cooling rack and cool completely in the pan. Cut out shapes with cookie cutters, or cut into squares.

**Makes about 16 bars.**

# May the Fudge Be with You

## INGREDIENTS

| | |
|---|---|
| 2 | tablespoons butter, plus more for greasing pan |
| 4 | cups superfine sugar* |
| 4 | ounces unsweetened chocolate, chopped |
| 1 | cup heavy cream, at room temperature |
| $1/2$ | teaspoon salt |
| 1 | teaspoon vanilla extract |

**1.** Grease a 9-by-13-inch baking pan.

**2.** Combine the sugar, chocolate, cream, and salt in a saucepan. Place the pan on the stove and switch on the heat to medium. Cook, stirring constantly, until the sugar is dissolved and the chocolate is melted. With adult help, clip a candy thermometer to the side of the pan. Let the mixture continue to cook without stirring until the thermometer reads 238°F. Remove the pan from the heat and add the 2 tablespoons butter and vanilla, stirring gently until combined.

**3.** Let the fudge cool, about 5 minutes. Beat the candy with the wooden spoon until it turns from glossy to dull. Pour the fudge into the greased pan and cool for 20 minutes. Cut into shapes or squares, then let the fudge cool completely.
**Makes about 16 pieces.**

*If you can't find superfine sugar, place the same amount of granulated sugar in a food processor and pulse several times.

# Mos Eisley Spacetortes

## CRUST

One 18-ounce package Oreo® cookies, finely crushed

8    ounces cream cheese, at room temperature

## FILLING

9    ounces chocolate, chopped (or $1^1/_2$ cups semisweet chocolate chips)

$1^1/_2$ cups creamy peanut butter

**1.** To make the crust, in a large bowl mix together the crushed cookies and the cream cheese with the wooden spoon until combined.
**2.** Set the cookie cutters on a baking sheet and lightly spray the inside and bottoms with vegetable-oil cooking spray. Press 2 tablespoons of the crust mixture into the bottom of each cutter. Chill in the refrigerator for 15 minutes.
**3.** To make the filling, stir together the chocolate and the peanut butter in a medium nonreactive metal bowl. Fill a saucepan about $1/_3$ with water. Set the pan on the stove and switch on the heat to medium so the water simmers. With adult help, set the bowl over the saucepan of simmering water and cook, stirring with the rubber spatula, until the chocolate and peanut butter are melted and smooth. Turn off the heat. Remove the bowl from the pan and stir for a minute or so to cool.
**4.** For each cookie cutter, pour the filling over the chilled crust to just under the top of the cookie cutter. Chill until the filling is set, about 1 hour. Gently remove the cookie cutters.
**5.** Repeat steps 2 and 4 with the remaining crust and filling.
**Makes 9 tortes.**

# Wookiee Pies

## COOKIES

| | |
|---|---|
| 1 2/3 | cups all-purpose flour |
| 2/3 | cup cocoa powder |
| 1 1/2 | teaspoons baking soda |
| 1/2 | teaspoon salt |
| 4 | tablespoons unsalted butter, at room temperature |
| 4 | tablespoons vegetable shortening |
| 1 | cup packed dark brown sugar |
| 1 | egg |
| 1 | teaspoon vanilla extract |
| 1 1/4 | cups milk, at room temperature |

**1.** Preheat the oven to 375°F.

**2.** Line 2 baking sheets with parchment paper. Using a black felt-tip marker, trace the cookie cutter shapes onto the parchment 48 times (trace 2 shapes for each pie), spacing the shapes at least 2 inches apart, to create the template. Flip the parchment over, so the pen markings are facedown on the baking sheet.

**3.** Sift together the flour, cocoa powder, baking soda, and salt onto a sheet of wax paper. In a bowl, beat together the butter, shortening, and brown sugar with the electric mixer on low speed until just combined. Increase the speed to medium and beat until fluffy and smooth, about 3 minutes. Add the egg and vanilla and beat for another 2 minutes.

**4.** Add half of the flour mixture and half of the milk to the batter and beat on low until just incorporated. Scrape down the sides of the bowl. Add the remaining flour mixture and milk and beat until completely combined.

**5.** Fit a pastry bag with a #10 round tip, and fill the bag with the batter. On both baking sheets, trace the shapes you made on the parchment with the batter, then fill in the middles.

*[continued]*

**6.** Bake 1 sheet at a time until the pies spring back when pressed gently, about 10 minutes.

**7.** Using pot holders, remove from the oven and let the cakes cool on the sheet for about 5 minutes before transferring them with a spatula to a cooling rack to cool completely. Top with filling as directed below.

## FILLING

| | |
|---|---|
| $1^1/_3$ cups | confectioners' sugar |
| $^1/_2$ cup | cocoa powder |
| 4 | tablespoons unsalted butter, at room temperature |
| 3 | tablespoons heavy cream |
| 1 | teaspoon vanilla extract |
| $^1/_2$ | teaspoon salt |

**1.** In a bowl, beat together the confectioners' sugar, cocoa, and butter with the electric mixer, starting on low speed and increasing to medium, until the mixture is crumbly, about 1 minute. Add the heavy cream, vanilla, and salt and beat on high until smooth, about 3 minutes.

**2.** Using a spatula or pastry bag, spread the flat side of one baked cake with the filling. Top with another cake of the same shape. Repeat with remaining cakes.

**Makes about 24 pies.**

# Jar Jar Fig Bars

## INGREDIENTS

| | |
|---|---|
| | Butter for greasing pan |
| 1 | cup dried figs, chopped |
| 1/2 | teaspoon all-purpose flour |
| 1 | cup creamy peanut butter |
| 1/4 | cup packed brown sugar |
| 2/3 | cup honey |
| 6 | cups of your favorite cereal or granola |
| 1 | teaspoon ground cinnamon |
| 1 | cup toasted pecans, chopped |

**1.** Lightly grease a 9-by-13-inch baking pan. Place the figs in a medium bowl. Sprinkle the flour over the figs and toss to coat. Set aside.

**2.** Put the peanut butter, sugar, and honey in a large pan or saucepan. Place the pan on the stove, switch on the heat to low, and cook, stirring, until smooth and simmering, about 10 minutes. Remove from the heat. Add the cereal, cinnamon, pecans, and figs, and stir until combined.

**3.** Press the mixture into the greased pan and chill 30 minutes or overnight. Cut out shapes with cookie cutters or cut into squares.

**Makes about 16 bars.**

# Skywalker Sugar Cookies

INGREDIENTS

| | |
|---|---|
| 1 | cup butter, at room temperature |
| 1 | cup sugar |
| 1 | egg |
| 1 | teaspoon vanilla extract |
| 3 | cups all-purpose flour, plus more for dusting work surface |
| 1/4 | teaspoon salt |
| 2 | teaspoons baking powder |

**1.** Preheat the oven to 350°F.

**2.** In a large bowl, beat the butter and sugar with the electric mixer on medium until fluffy. Add the egg and vanilla and mix to combine. In another bowl, mix together the 3 cups flour, salt, and baking powder. Add the dry ingredients to the butter mixture, 1 cup at a time, mixing completely after each addition.

**3.** Turn the dough out onto a floured surface and knead a few times until smooth. Divide the dough in half, setting 1 portion aside. Roll out the dough ⅛ inch thick with the rolling pin, sprinkling with flour as needed. Cut out shapes with the cookie cutters. Gather up the dough scraps, roll them out again, and cut out more cookies. Repeat with the remaining half of the dough.

**4.** Bake the cookies on an ungreased baking sheet until lightly golden, 7 to 9 minutes. Remove the cookies with a spatula to cooling rack to cool completely.

**5.** Decorate with icing as directed on page 62.

**Makes about 4 dozen cookies.**

*[continued]*

## ROYAL ICING

| 2 | egg whites |
| 1 | teaspoons fresh lemon juice |
| 1 | teaspoon vanilla extract |
| 3 | cups confectioners' sugar, plus more if needed |
|   | Food coloring (optional) |

**1.** In a large bowl, beat the egg whites with the electric mixer on high speed until foamy. Add the lemon juice and vanilla and beat until soft peaks form. Gradually add the confectioners' sugar and beat until the frosting is stiff and fluffy. If it is too stiff, add water $1/2$ teaspoon at a time to thin. If it is too thin, add additional confectioners' sugar 1 tablespoon at a time until it is of piping consistency. (Royal Icing hardens very quickly. Keep the bowl covered with a damp cloth or paper towel while you are working.)

**2.** To color the icing, remove a small amount to another bowl and add drops of food coloring until you reach the desired shade. Stir until the coloring is uniformly blended.

**3.** To ice the entire surface of the cookie, fill a pastry bag fit with a #3 tip and pipe around the edge of the cookies with the icing. Let the icing set until dry to the touch, about 20 minutes. Thin out more of the Royal Icing by adding water a teaspoon at a time until it pours easily from a spoon. Fill another pastry bag fitted with a #3 round tip with the thinned icing and fill in between the lines of the icing outline. Pop any air bubbles with a toothpick. Allow to dry at least 2 hours.

**4.** To add detail, fill a pastry bag fitted with a #3 round tip with a contrasting color of icing and follow the templates on facing page.

## YODA

| 1 | green background and detail |
| 2 | white detail |
| 3 | black detail |

## R2-D2

| white background | 1 |
| gray detail | 2 |
| blue detail | 3 |
| black detail | 4 |
| red detail | 5 |

## DARTH VADER

| 1 | black background and detail |
| 2 | white detail |

# Icing Suggestions

# Index